Where Does the Teacher Live?

by Paula Kurzband Feder

pictures by Lillian Hoban

DUTTON CHILDREN'S BOOKS
NEW YORK

Unicorn is a registered trademark of Dutton Children's Books.
Library of Congress number 78-13157
ISBN 0-525-44889-6
Published in the United States by Dutton Children's Books,
a division of Penguin Books USA Inc.
375 Hudson Street, New York, New York 10014
Editor: Ann Durell   Designer: Riki Levinson

to my daughter, Sarah Eleanore

It was Monday morning.

The children in Class 2–3

were having their milk.

Alba was sitting next to

her best friend, Nancy.

"Nancy," said Alba,

"do you know where

Mrs. Greengrass lives?"

Mrs. Greengrass was

the teacher of Class 2–3.

"She lives in school,"

said Nancy. "All the teachers

live in school."

6

Willie was sitting behind them.

"Oh no no no," said Willie.

"She lives in a house

just like we do."

Willie was the

smartest boy in the class.

"Maybe Willie is right,"

said Alba.

"Let's find out," said Willie.

"We can wait after school

and see where she goes."

"Oh, she won't ever come out,"

said Nancy.

At three o'clock,

Alba, Willie, and Nancy

waited in front of the school.

Mrs. Greengrass came out.

She did not see the children.

They were hiding behind

a big boxwood bush.

"See?" said Alba to Nancy.

"Willie was right.

Mrs. Greengrass does not

live in school."

They followed Mrs. Greengrass

down the street,

across the avenue,

and along the park.

12

Then she crossed another street.

"My mother will not let me

cross any more streets,"

said Nancy.

"All right," said Alba.

"We can just watch."

A bus stopped.

Mrs. Greengrass got on.

The bus went up the street
and turned at the corner.

"She must live far away,"
said Alba.

"Maybe she lives in
the country," said Nancy.

"Oh no," said Willie.
"That was a city bus.
She must live in the city."

"Maybe Willie is right,"
said Alba.

"This is fun," said Willie.

"Let's do it again tomorrow."

At three o'clock on Tuesday,

Alba, Willie, and Nancy

hid behind the boxwood bush

to wait for Mrs. Greengrass.

"Look," said Willie.

"She is walking the same way.

She is going to take

the bus again."

They followed Mrs. Greengrass

down the street,

across the avenue,

and along the park.

They watched her

cross the street.

A bus went in front of her.

"I told you,"

said Willie.

Then the bus moved away.

Surprise! Mrs. Greengrass

was still there.

She was still walking.

"Willie," said Alba,

"you were wrong."

"Maybe she is not

going home today," said Willie.

"Maybe she can walk
to her house," said Alba.

"Maybe she can
walk ten miles,"
said Nancy.

"No one can walk ten miles,"
said Willie.

"Maybe she can,"
said Alba.
"You were wrong today.
She did not take the bus."

Mrs. Greengrass kept on walking.
She went around the corner.
They could not see her anymore.

The next day was Wednesday.

It was raining hard.

"Here comes Mrs. Greengrass,"
said Alba.

"She cannot walk home today,"
said Willie. "It is too wet."

Mrs. Greengrass came
down the steps.
She looked
to the left.
She looked
to the right.

Suddenly

she put her hand up

in the air.

"Look," said Willie.

"A taxi is stopping for her."

Mrs. Greengrass got in the taxi.

Alba, Willie, and Nancy

waited to see which way

the taxi went.

It went the same way

as the bus.

"Mrs. Greengrass has many ways

of going home," said Willie.

"I know something," said Alba.

"Mrs. Greengrass lives

on the west side of the city.

This is the east side,

and she always goes

the other way."

"I am getting all wet,"
said Nancy, "and I am
getting tired of this. Tomorrow
let us ask Mrs. Greengrass
where she lives."

"Oh no! Wait one more day,"

said Alba. "This is a

big mystery."

"And we are good detectives,"

said Willie.

"Okay, one more day," said Nancy.

So on Thursday,

Alba, Willie, and Nancy

waited for Mrs. Greengrass.

She came out of the school.

She just stood there.

She did not walk.

She did not get on a bus.

She did not take a taxi.

A blue car came up the street.

A woman was driving the car.

She said hello to Mrs. Greengrass.

"Mrs. Greengrass

is getting into the car,"

said Nancy.

The blue car drove away.

"It is not going the same way

as the bus and taxi," said Alba.

"It is not going the same way

that Mrs. Greengrass walked,"

said Willie.

"I am all mixed up," said Alba.

"Tomorrow we will ask

Mrs. Greengrass where she lives."

On Friday,

Alba, Willie, and Nancy

were eating lunch.

Mrs. Greengrass came into

the lunchroom.

"Mrs. Greengrass!"

they shouted.

The teacher came

over to them.

"Mrs. Greengrass,

where do you live?"

asked Alba.

"Do you live in school?"

asked Nancy.

"Do you live in the city?"

asked Willie.

"So many questions,"

said Mrs. Greengrass.

"Why do you want to know?"

"We just wondered," said Alba.

"We followed you,"
said Willie. "On Monday
we saw you take a bus."

"On Tuesday we saw you walk,"
said Nancy. "You walked
the same way as the bus."

"On Wednesday we saw you
take a taxi," said Willie. "It went
the same way as the bus."

"I live on the west side,"

said Mrs. Greengrass.

"See? I told you she lived

on the west side,"

said Alba to Willie.

"But yesterday
you got a ride in a car,"
said Nancy.

"The car went a different way,"
said Willie.

"You are good detectives,"
said Mrs. Greengrass.
"Yesterday my friend
drove me to her house
for dinner."

She smiled.
"Today I am going home
another way. Wait for me
after school."

At three o'clock,

Alba, Willie, and Nancy

stood in front of the school.

"Maybe she will fly home

in a helicopter,"

said Nancy.

Mrs. Greengrass

came out of the school.

"Hello, children," she said.

A small truck stopped

in front of the school.

39

A man was driving the truck.

Mrs. Greengrass said,

"Children, this is my uncle,

Frank Greengrass.

He sells ice cream

to the stores."

Frank Greengrass

climbed out of the truck.

He gave something

to Mrs. Greengrass.

Mrs. Greengrass

walked over to the children.

"Here are three
chocolate marshmallow
ice-cream pops," she said.
"You are all
such good detectives."

42

And Alba, Nancy, Willie,
and Mrs. Greengrass went home
in the ice-cream truck.